The Tale of Tully and Juno

Sarah Menary

With illustrations by Caroline Freaney

Published in 2005 by Sparky Press
15 Bedford Street, Berkhamsted, HP4 2EN
www.tullyandjuno.com

ISBN 0-9550651-0-0

Typeset by Sandra Smith, Rosewood Publishing, Berkhamsted
Printed and bound in Great Britain by The Cromwell Press, Trowbridge.

This book is dedicated to Tully and Juno

Tully and Juno's birth certificate

D.O.B. 5 April '01

Mum: Bagheera

G. Mum: Bess

GG Mum: Izzie

GGG Mum: Bumble

GGGG Mum: Bella

*****

Wormed with liquid Panacur 26 April

Chapter One

There is a winding road, in fact more of a rough track, that leads to the cottage. One moment you are in amongst the houses of Chorley Wood and then, if you take a left turn down Beggars Lane, you suddenly find yourself in a private park. The park has green pastures on either side, which are protected behind lines of great oak trees. Nothing can be seen beyond and, as you continue up the track, the sounds of the road suddenly vanish.

Imagine it is March, the time when summer begins to think about joining the year – when wildlife stirs and the heavy yoke of cold and fog lifts. Through a series of winding turns you can reach the cottage with its white, stone walls. It sits on the other side of a small humpback bridge with a gurgling brook running beneath. The windows have old diamond-shaped panes. White wooden trellises strung with rose plants, not yet in bud, stand outside the house. The arch of the stone doorway comes to a point at the top, and the door itself is made of thick, dark wood that has survived many summers and winters.

Inside you find smooth stone slabs on the floor and the windows are small, white arches matching the doorway. To the right-hand side of the hallway there is an old sofa with

great wooden, curling arms and faded green, velvet cushions. That is where Bagheera and her kittens used to rest, and this is where the tale of Tully and Juno begins.

Bagheera was named after the clever panther from a story called The Jungle Book and it is easy to see why – she has sleek, short black hair, with long legs, a long tail and almond-shaped eyes. She is thought by the other animals in the cottage to be one of the most intelligent, and that is why it surprised them when she fell foul of a treacherous wild cat.

In the cottage there lived three cats, all female including Bagheera, her mother Bess and her grandmother Izzie. There were also two black Labradors – named George and Mildred – and outside lived a whole host of ducks and geese. Two humans lived in the cottage and made sure the animals had food to eat, although there was never quite enough to go round. They lived very simply but all were happy to be in such a beautiful place.

Bagheera knew she was a striking cat; she had heard the humans talking about how she looked like the ancient figure of the Egyptian cat god, Bastet. Naturally she longed for romance. But there were no male cats at the cottage and she had been brought up by her mother Bess to expect no children as there already were too many mouths to feed. So while life at the cottage might be called idyllic, for a restless soul like Bagheera's there was something missing.

One day a male cat began hanging around the outskirts of the cottage garden. The news of his arrival rapidly passed

The cottage near Chorley Wood

from duck to goose to cat to Labrador. The newcomer had wild, long hair and, as the animals said to each other in a hushed whisper, was what you would call "feral" (meaning wild). Most British cats these days are "domesticated" which means that they are brought up by and looked after by humans, rather than fending for themselves in the wild. Domestic cats very rarely, if at all, come into contact with feral cats and there is naturally much curiosity when this happens. After all, feral cats are the "original" cats and stories of their fierceness, independence and amazing hunting skills have been woven into tales. These have been passed down from mother to kitten for many generations. Feral cats are even more mysterious, Bagheera mused, as they have no human name, since they are not owned or cared for by humans. As the cat daily surveyed their cottage from a distance, Bagheera began to watch him.

She was accustomed to going for long walks over the humpback bridge and into the pastures alongside the track that led to the cottage. It was the time of year when butterflies begin to appear, and much fun could be had leaping up and trying to catch their rainbow wings. She knew that he was watching her too, and her mother had warned her that on no account should she go near him. But she would not alter her usual routine – after all it was her home and not his.

One day she was heading back towards the cottage when she heard a strange call like nothing she had heard before. While she was standing, still listening and not quite ready to leave, the cat suddenly appeared from behind a tree and leant

against the trunk. "That is the sound my type of cat makes when we see a beauty such as yourself. Will you walk with me a while and let me tell you about the way we wild cats live?" said he, stroking his black furry moustache and whiskers. He had a long, black coat, which was thick with white stripey markings and so very glossy. Bagheera was surprised he could keep himself in such good condition while living outdoors all the time.

She had a hunger for knowledge and could imagine herself passing on the tales of the wild cat to the other animals in the winter evenings, which always passed so slowly, but she knew that this was not the only reason she had accepted his invitation. And so they walked and talked – he explaining his solitary life as a wild cat, his hunting skills, the many courageous battles he had fought against dogs, foxes and other wild cats, and what it was like to wake up in a new place each day and encounter new adventures.

At the end of their walk, he asked her if she would meet him the next day at the same time and place. He added that he was lonely and that he had enjoyed her company very much. Bagheera did not think of declining: the afternoon had been such fun. She went to the cottage with her tail held high, leaping down the track with excitement.

She knew Bess would not approve but she did not lie to her mother. Instead, she decided to tell her what had occurred. Once she told the tales to the other animals, she was sure her mother would ache to know more of the wild cat's life,

just as she did.

Indeed Bess did not approve. "I warn you my daughter that no good will come of this," she said shaking her paw at Bagheera. "You know you must not have relations with a male cat as we have so many mouths to feed. Have I not told you before how ruthless feral males are – they not only attack their own kind but they are tied to no place and care not what they leave behind."

That night Bagheera passed on the wild cat's stories to George and Mildred, and even the ducks and geese crowded into the cottage to hear. She enjoyed the attention of all the animals and found she was a good storyteller.

The next day, and for days after that, Bagheera took long walks with the feral male. One day he paused in the middle of a story and looked her in the eyes with great intensity.

"Bagheera, mine is a solitary life as you well know," he said softly. "As you are interested in my life, I too am interested in yours. I have travelled far and seen many things but I feel now that I need to settle. I am tired of wandering and I wish to make a life in this place with you. I can think of no finer cat than yourself to spend my time with – you are indeed beautiful, agile and intelligent, and I look forward to our walks with great longing. I know that the cottage cannot support another soul, and if you and I have kittens there would be many more mouths to feed. But I am a great hunter and I can provide for many with my skills. Your family need not rely on

the humans alone, and I can bring the little ones up to hunt like me. What say you – my love – Bagheera?"

Bagheera was astonished by what she heard, and yet it fulfilled her secret hopes that had been steadily growing as she spent each day with the wild cat. She did not think her mother would agree to the union but Bagheera was now grown up, and it is part of their lore that when kittens can no longer be picked up by the scruff of their neck the mother no longer has control of them. Yet theirs was an unusual situation, as Bagheera lived with her mother and her grandmother, so it was harder to disregard their wishes and she had no desire to do so.

Although Bagheera knew that her mother was wise, she reasoned that her mother had not spent time with the feral male, heard his thoughts, grown to know him as she had done. His proposal had been very proper – he was concerned about feeding any kittens that might arrive, and his suggestion that he might hunt to provide for them showed his responsible nature, however unlikely that might be in a wild cat. Was it not possible that she, beautiful Bagheera, had been especially fortunate?

And so Bagheera accepted his proposal, and he hunted that very afternoon to give Bess an offering of food, so as to make things easier between them. Bess's paws twitched when she heard the news, but she realised there was nothing she could do and gave her daughter a tender lick. It was then that the wild cat came into the house with his offering, and from then on he became a member of the household.

A couple of weeks passed and Bagheera was very happy. She would spend hours curled up with the wild cat smelling the scent of woodlands in his fur. He took over the role of storyteller and evenings were joyful occasions when all the animals gathered round to hear his tales. Soon Bagheera was expecting kittens and this was everything she hoped for. Bess and Izzie were excited about nursing the kittens and having such young ones playing in the cottage once again.

There were six kittens in the litter when Bagheera gave birth. Each could easily fit into the palm of your hand. Some had Bagheera's short black hair and some had the wild cat's long, thick hair. And in this litter were Tully and Juno. Tully had a very long, fluffy coat that was black from the top of his head, down his back to the tip of his bushy tail. His chest and belly were white and he had a pure white flash in the middle of his forehead that ran down his nose, above his mouth and across his cheeks. The flash was paired with very long white whiskers, and the combination made him look like he had an enormous, white moustache that curled up at either end. Around his pale green eyes, forehead and ears he was black again, except for the long white hairs peeking out of his ears. His front and back legs were black but his paws were all white, which made them look rather large.

Juno looked much like her mother, with her almond-shaped eyes that were pale blue to begin with but turned a dark amber after a few weeks. At first sight she seemed black, but there was a hint of chocolate brown that could be seen

especially well when the sunlight filtered through the window next to the green sofa, where the kittens lay with their mother. Juno was probably the smallest kitten and Tully the largest – where he was fluffy and a hotchpotch of black and white, she was sleek and black all over. But she did have a few features from her feral father – under her front legs there was a little white fur, like underarm hair, and also a dab of white fur right in the centre of her chest.

Almost immediately Juno helped take care of her brother by grooming him – licking his fur steadily and slowly all over, particularly behind the ears. Perhaps she was copying Bagheera who was busy attending to all her offspring. Tully was always the first to take his feed and the first to go to sleep. Juno was a little anxious right from the start and would keep a lookout, but along with her siblings, she felt mostly safe and cosseted next to her mother's belly. Several happy weeks passed for the kittens.

And then one day, the wild cat disappeared. Since Bagheera had given birth, she had not been as aware of his movements. He left late each night to go hunting and could usually be found the following morning sleeping in one of the armchairs next to the sofa. That morning Bagheera woke up and his chair was empty. She wondered where he was and left the kittens sleeping on the sofa while she went outside to look for him. Hours passed and he did not return. She asked all the ducks and geese whether they had seen anything during the night, but none reported any strange happenings. Hours

turned into days, and the atmosphere in the cottage became gloomy. Bess said nothing but it was clear what she was thinking – that the wild cat had abandoned Bagheera and her kittens. Who knows what really happened? It is possible that something had happened to him while hunting, but there was no way of knowing. Although Bagheera kept hoping for some news, she never saw or heard of him again.

And so the time came, when the kittens were about five weeks old and would soon require more than their mother's milk to survive, that Bess spoke to her daughter about the future and what the humans were planning.

Chapter Two

Bess had overheard the humans answering the telephone – the words “four boys, two girls” … “£40 each” … “ready in June” were heard several times and could only mean one thing: that the kittens were to be sold one by one and would shortly leave for other homes. Although Bagheera knew that most mother cats watch their kittens leave and never see them growing up, it did not make it any easier to bear – somehow she thought that things would have turned out otherwise for her. Had she not been with her mother and grandmother all her life? But as Bess and Izzie gently told Bagheera, her chief concern must be to ensure her kittens had enough food.

“Humans are good carers,” said Izzie. “Our little ones will surely find good homes where they will always be provided for. You must present yourself and the kittens well to the humans who will come to look at them. Show them what a lovely litter you have and what a healthy, caring mother you are. We cannot let even one be left behind as it will be better off not being here. That is your responsibility now, Bagheera.”

Then Bess and Izzie curled on the sofa with Bagheera, who was weak with worried emotion, to comfort her. By the time she woke up to give the kittens their feed, she realised

with a heavy heart that her mother and grandmother were right. She would prepare for the strangers' visits by carefully washing each kitten all over and feeding them beforehand, so that they would be at their most happy and contented when they were viewed.

The first stranger was a lady wearing a lavender, cashmere shawl with her long fingernails painted to match. Juno was laying with her feet against her mother and her face pointing outward towards the lady. She rolled on her back to stretch and with her upturned face and contented expression she seemed to be reaching out with her soft amber eyes and tiny, elegant paws. She was the first to be picked up and inspected. The lady then inspected each kitten, considering their attributes, but Juno was her final choice.

The next day a young couple peered down at the litter, marvelling at the entire kitten family cuddled up to their mother's tummy. They were impressed that Bagheera's mother Bess and her grandmother Izzie still remained at the cottage as well. They picked out Tully, who had supped more of his mother's milk than the rest, and as a result was very dozy. They pointed out to each other his enormous milky moustache and sleepy eyes, and this is what led them to choose him. Then other humans came and chose the remaining kittens. And so money changed hands and dates were set for Tully, Juno and their brothers and sisters to be collected. Due to their interest in the kitten's ancestry, Tully's new owners were also given a piece of notepaper which acted as a birth certificate for all the

kittens in the litter. On it Bagheera's owners had written down a kind of family tree, which you may have noticed at the beginning of this book.

Bagheera savoured every moment left tending her kittens. She wished she could tell them what was happening and prepare them for their new lives, but they were too small to understand.

About three weeks later, each day seemed to bring a new car to the cottage and a rap on the old door. A few minutes later there would be one less kitten. When the lady with the lavender shawl came to collect Juno, she was nowhere to be found and some considerable time was spent finding her. It turned out she was hiding in a drainpipe – did she realise what was about to happen or was it her adventurous nature (of which we will hear more later)? She found the journey very upsetting and struggled to break free of her wicker cat carrier. Luckily she did not have to travel far that day. In fact, her new home was in Chorley Wood.

The lady lived in part of an old town house, and had renovated the interior so that it was a mixture of wooden beams and white plaster with modern furnishings. In the sitting room a square, glass coffee table, covered in shiny books, sat in front of a white sofa and carpet. The whole place was strikingly light, immaculate and luxurious – a contrast with the worn sofa, cool flagstones and the uneven sunlight which filtered through the diamond windowpanes of the cottage.

Meanwhile Tully's skill for sleeping meant that he had

a very uneventful journey to his new home. This was about an hour away in a town called Berkhamsted (which the locals fondly refer to as "Berko"). Tully and the couple arrived at a small, terraced house on Bedford Street. At the end of the street, there was a canal bordered by flowers, rushes and trees.

When the grilled gate of the cat carrier swung down, Tully was still sleeping, curled up like a conch shell with his paw over his nose. His new owners reached for him and placed him down in the kitchen. From there he could see the conservatory in front of him, leading to a small garden beyond, and behind him was the sitting room. He was shown his personal food and water bowls (white and blue pottery with a fish bone painted on the side), his indoor toilet and, best of all, a wicker basket with furry, cream wool bedding just as soft as his mother's tummy.

He quickly discovered that his new owners liked playing with him and would try to get him to sit on their laps. Tully rather liked all the attention and it was not long before they were all sitting close together on the sofa. It was often a rather messy house but no less comfortable for that, and he enjoyed searching out a new, private sleeping spot every day – a favourite was a sock draw in the bedroom dresser, which was missing its front.

Juno also found that all preparations for her arrival had been made, with a purple velour-lined basket and some steel, shiny feeding bowls. But the first night was long and difficult. She paced around mewing sadly, searching for her mother and

Tully curled up like a conch shell

brothers and sister, not understanding why they were not there. For the first couple of weeks she kept more than a polite distance from her new owner. Gradually the relationship improved, helped along by occasional bowls of cream and deluxe kitten pâtés "for the discerning owner". But she was still lonely, as the lady was out a lot of the time, and there were no other animals or toys to play with. Juno found she could never exhaust herself and was always watching, waiting and hoping for something exciting to happen. This desire for excitement and activity led to a few unfortunate incidents where the lady would return to find Juno sitting on the stairs with wild, wide eyes and ears pointed back. Often the results of her afternoon adventures were strewn across the sitting room: chewed tassels on the sofa cushions, a number of ornaments lying on the floor or even some pulled threads in the curtains from Juno's mountain climbing activity! Because of this, the lady brought a scratching post, a ball with a bell inside and a furry mouse-toy.

At this age both Tully and Juno were too young to go outside, but as the weeks passed and they grew bigger, their respective homes began to seem small and confined where once they had seemed very large. Tully was taken outside for the first time when he was four months old – the couple threw back the conservatory doors, and as he made his first tentative steps out, he breathed in the scent of grass mingled with flowers, soil and tree bark. Birds called out to each other from the trees, which made his ears twitch excitedly. His eyes grew

Juno kept more than a polite distance...

wide at the many ants and insects before him – which should he catch first? The lawn had not been mown for some time, creating a jungle-like effect for a kitten his size. He galloped across the lawn as if he were a lion in the tall grasses of an African plain, and then lay on his front paws waiting to pounce. This was the beginning of how Tully learnt his hunting skills.

Juno, meanwhile, never got the chance to explore the outside of the house in Chorley Wood. Instead, she and her owner's possessions were being packed up ready to travel to Paris of all places! While Tully settled into his new Berko home, Juno was being shipped off to a new one far away. Just as the lady had her passport, so Juno had her own "pet passport". The journey was a long one – first the train to London, then a taxi ride to Waterloo station, where they boarded the Eurostar train to the centre of Paris, and then another taxi… until Juno and the lady finally arrived at an *apartement*: a small flat in a wealthy avenue of the city.

Chapter Three

Tully and Juno's lives were as different as they could be. Tully spent his days concentrating on three activities: sleeping blissfully in assorted places (not least spread-eagled across the man's chest while he was lying on his back), eating as much food as possible (other food bowls in the neighbourhood were investigated as well as his own), and exploring the many gardens that led from his home. There were no field mice to be found in a town like Berkhamsted, so he developed a taste for catching canal frogs, and proudly positioned these in the sitting room to greet his owners on their return!

Juno spent her days in the very smart apartement. Cocktail and dinner parties were a frequent occurrence. After a few weeks her owner bought a cat harness so that Juno could be taken for walks in the streets of Paris. The first time she was put into the harness she struggled violently and became tangled up in the various straps, but she soon realised that it was her ticket to the outside world which she craved to explore. As you know by now, Juno was as adventurous as she was anxious, and perhaps her owner was not so wrong to use the harness. The chaotic sounds of the city were likely to make any cat bolt, especially one of a nervous disposition. And so began Juno's society life – she would accompany her owner to

the various brasseries and cafés in Paris, sometimes sitting on the lady's lap to lick some ice cream out of a silver cup.

On the anniversary of the day she left the cottage, Juno was given a black velvet collar, studded with diamante crystals that sparkled when they caught the light. This was to replace the harness and had a small gold tag with her address and telephone number, in case she ever became lost. She was now free to walk the streets on her own, and had her own cat door to come and go as she pleased. But the collar was not only to identify her – it was also a fashion accessory, and Juno was now as well dressed as her owner! Losing the harness and gaining such an ornament (which turned the heads of all the cats in the district) gave her new confidence and, much like her mother, Juno developed an elegant, slightly swaying trot with her tail held high as she sashayed down the long, wide avenues of Paris.

It was shortly after this that she was spotted in a café near the Champs Elysées. Juno's owner was given a business card by a woman at another table. This person was the editor of a lifestyle magazine, which had a page in each issue featuring luxury pet accessories. She remarked on Juno's sleek fur, her long, tapered legs and her almond eyes. She said that Juno looked like a cat version of a 1950s movie star called Audrey Hepburn.

A few days later she was taken to a loft apartment in Montmartre (where all the artists live). It turned out to be a photographic studio. The walls and floor were white and there

were lots of lamps on high stands. Some men brought in a purple, watered silk *chaise longue* – which is like a small sofa that curls over at one end.

Juno was photographed wearing her diamante collar, lying down on her belly but sitting up on her front paws, with her face turned towards the camera. Sitting next to her was a young woman with a shiny black, fringed bob, wearing a gold, satin evening dress and gloves with a large diamante bracelet over the top of each one. The model held a full champagne flute in her hand. A small, round, ebony table, inlaid with mother of pearl, was placed at the side, on which there was a black invitation card engraved with gold writing. The caption for the picture was "Et maintenant, les mademoiselles sont prêt pour un soir de Paris" ("And now the young ladies are ready for a Paris evening").

And so this was the beginning of Juno's career as a Parisien cat model. She enjoyed the careful grooming she received before each photo-shoot, and was pleased with the results. She developed a very fine view of herself, and it was noticeable that she held her delicate chin just a little bit higher than before, as she sauntered home with her owner. She would pretend not to notice the other cats she trotted by, but secretly spied out of the corner of her eye whether they had noticed her. Her owner was paid well for her work and, in recognition of this contribution to the household, Juno was treated to the same food as the lady. Pieces of sirloin steak, wild salmon and even crème brulée were regular parts of her diet.

Perhaps the pinnacle of her modelling career was when she took to the catwalk with the famous human model, Bijou. A catwalk, in case you don't know, is the name given to the long platform that models walk up and down at fashion shows. Juno wore a shocking pink, suede cat harness with pure gold buckles, and Bijou wore a pink suede miniskirt and jacket with thigh-high matching boots. Bijou had straight, shoulder length black hair and a straight fringe that finished just above her eyebrows. She had a large, angular nose that was unusual for a model. Her name was also rather unexpected. Bijou in French means "jewel", and is often used to describe something which is small but beautiful. However, the model Bijou was immensely tall – if she were a jewel, then she would be one of the world's biggest but most finely cut diamonds. Her body was a tall, swaying column with each limb a long and elegant extension. Juno was tiny in comparison and the harness had to be specially made with a lead long enough to reach from Bijou's hand to Juno's back. At the end of the catwalk, Bijou was to stand with one hand on her left hip and her right leg resting on the heel of her boot and facing slightly out to the side, with her face turned fiercely forward. Juno was trained to sit at the same moment beside Bijou with her left front leg placed in front of her right.

Bijou had an exceptionally long stride for a female human. This made it difficult for Juno to keep up with her, so they had to practise many times. The day of the fashion show came and the backstage area was very cluttered and noisy.

There were racks and racks of clothes and the hairdressers, make-up artists, designers and models were all in a buzz of activity and anticipation. Juno's coat was prepared with an oil that made it especially sleek and shiny, and then she was fitted with the pink suede harness. Both models knew the moment had come when they heard the song called "Volare" and took to the catwalk.

There must have been two thousand people in the audience, many of them photographers. CLICK CLICK CLICK FLASH FLASH FLASH. Nothing had prepared Juno for the forest of flashbulbs that shot out bright bolts of light and heat. If you had been very close to Juno, you would have been able to see her fur slightly trembling. But she kept her eyes fixed on the end of the catwalk, and when Bijou stopped she placed her leg in front, with a slight flourish, and fixed the audience with the intense stare that models tend to use.

Being a cat model was not easy – yes, there were many assistants tending Juno's every need and she enjoyed being the centre of attention – but it could be nerve-wracking as well. The atmosphere in a studio or at a fashion show is hot and stuffy, with long periods spent waiting around. Many times Juno longed to go outside for some fresh, cool air. In addition to this she spent all her time with humans, and so you might say it was a lonely life for a young cat to live, without any feline friends.

Whilst Juno was spending her days modelling in the great city of Paris, Tully was living a much more humble life:

fishing for frogs, mostly given a simple diet of dry food by his owners – which he did his best to supplement with choicer offerings elsewhere – and sleeping. His fur had now grown very long, and was slightly wavy and shaggy. His front paws were like white boxing gloves – twice the size of Juno's paws - and he had very big, white back feet too – but the size of his paws were balanced by a thick and long shaggy tail which became an enormous swaying plume when he walked. The length of his fur over his legs made him look a little like he was wearing wide, baggy trousers. Around his neck he had developed a thick white ruff, like a lion's mane.

Tully was a strong, muscular cat who made stealthy and fierce attacks on the frogs of Berko, but though a hunter, he was distinguished most by his gentleness. He loved to give attention and to receive it from other cats and humans. This made him many good friends and he too became, in a local way, a bit of a celebrity.

And now we leave Tully and Juno for a while and turn to their Great Uncle Tully, whose story is, indeed, their story too.

Chapter Four

Deep in a forest near Chorley Wood there is another cottage, which is known as a "writer's retreat". It is a place where authors and poets go on their own to write, where there is no telephone, television, radio or other contact with the outside world. Water has to be drawn from a well, and the only heat comes from making a fire in the fireplace set deep into the wall of the sitting room. Apart from the sitting room, which is also a kitchen and where there is a worn oak table for writing and eating, there is a tiny bedroom and bathroom. One summer, ten years before Tully and Juno were settled into their lives, a man had gone to the cottage to write a book. He woke at dawn each day, drew water from the well, and ate his breakfast sitting on the doorstep listening to the bird song. Then he would go for a walk through the forest before sitting down to write. He became aware that he was not alone on his walks – there was a stirring in the undergrowth that seemed to mirror his steps, and occasionally he thought he saw a flash of ginger-brown fur caught by a shaft of sunlight coming down through the trees.

After a few weeks, the summer had ripened and the days were very warm and sunny. The man set up a small table outside, under the shade of an apple tree, and had the

occasional bite of bread and cheese while he passed the day writing. One day he left the table for a moment to bring out some water and a little wine, and when he returned he found a large, long-haired ginger cat eating the cheese! The cat was a Tom Cat, and these grow much bigger than normal domesticated males. Tully and Juno's feral father had been a Tom Cat also. The man's first impulse was to shoo the cat away, but the large size and majesty of the creature made him wait. In the end he walked over very slowly and quietly to get a better look. But the Tom's senses were finely tuned and, within an instant of the first step, the cat leapt off the table, raced through the undergrowth and disappeared. The man decided to see if he could tempt the cat back. Each day he went into the cottage at the same time and a dish with small pieces of cheese was left on the ground. He peered out from the small cottage window and waited to see what would happen.

The shaggy-haired, dark ginger Tom was planning his course of action equally carefully. For several days he crawled on his belly through the undergrowth and, hidden from sight, surveyed the scene through the tall grass. Each day he moved slightly further in and, just when the man had begun to give up ever seeing him again, he made his move. The man was washing some dishes in the sink when he looked out to see the cat eating the cheese. He resisted the urge to go outside to see better. He decided to leave the cheese each day and see if he might be able to build up the cat's trust, so that perhaps they could sit outside and eat their lunch together. Being alone to

write for the whole of the summer was exactly what the man wanted, free to think and imagine uninterrupted. But the companionship of an animal would be very welcome. It took a few days but eventually the cat's plate was moved near the man's feet, and the Tom was content to eat so close. As the weeks passed the cat confidently began to investigate inside the cottage and before long they were sharing the cottage too.

When the summer drew to a close, it was time for the writer to pack his things and make the journey home. He had grown very attached to the ginger Tom and wondered if it would be cruel to try and bring the cat with him to his home. On the last night he spoke aloud these thoughts, pretending that the cat could understand him.

Shortly afterwards these words rang out, almost as if they were in his head:

"Why, I rather like the idea and, if it does not suit me, can we agree that you will drive me back to this forest?"

The man was not sure what had happened. Cats could not speak. He had not seen the cat's mouth move. The only way to test his senses was to continue the conversation. The man said, "Would you like to know about Bridgewater House, where I live?"

"Yes, every detail," said the Tom. "I imagine you will describe it very well as you are writer."

So for the rest of the evening the man carefully described his house – its position next to the canal lock and a pub called "The Boat"; the garden running alongside the canal

with foxgloves and hollyhocks; the round, white table made of fancy ironwork with two chairs where he would sit when he wrote outside; the three floors of the house with the top floor an airy gallery with six, tall windows and a balcony; the slate roof and the eaves of the house with wooden scroll carving; the conservatory with its wicker chairs with soft, floral cushions and the tall shiny, green plants in clay pots. The Tom Cat made the occasional comment or nod. The cat then set down one condition in return for accompanying the writer: he must not tell anyone else that the cat could speak. This the man accepted.

When the man woke in the morning, the cat was nowhere to be seen. Although this did not differ from their normal routine, he began to wonder as he warmed the kettle for his tea, whether the whole thing had been his invention, brought on by too much seclusion from other humans. He packed his things and then cleaned the cottage – so that it was ready for another writer – and made his way out to his car. It was time to leave and he felt increasingly heavy with disappointment when he saw no sign of the ginger Tom. He decided to have a brief look around the outside of the cottage, but there was no sign of him. Getting into the driving seat of the car, he found the Tom right beside him, sitting upright in the passenger seat!

"You look surprised to see me," the cat said.

"Well, yes I am. I had thought last night was all my imagining but here you are. Are you ready to leave the forest?"

Bridgewater House

"Yes, I like an adventure and I have become rather accustomed to the comforts of a home."

"My name is Richard Lebowski. What shall I call you? What is your name?"

"I do not have a name, I have no need for one."

"I think it would be useful for us now that we are talking to each other. How would you feel if I suggested a name?"

"By all means. Have you anything in mind?"

The writer thought for a minute. What would be a fitting name for this strong, noble and truly remarkable cat? He scanned his mind, thinking of famous writers and figures from the past. He had a particular love of the classical world – ancient Greece and Rome and he admired the Roman writer Cicero. It seemed a little pompous to call the ginger Tom Cicero; he could not imagine doing that. But Cicero had a middle name, Tullius, that seemed more fitting. "I would like to call you Tullius."

And so they set off in the car. Tullius – although he tried not show to it – became a little nervous and decided to lie flat and sink his claws into the car seat, to hang on as the car followed the twists of the road. The journey took about an hour and of all places it was Berkhamsted that the writer lived! And so ten years earlier than our kitten Tully reached the town from Bagheera's cottage in Chorley Wood, Great Uncle Tullius had made much the same journey. Richard's house by the canal is only a few minutes walk from the terraced house where the

Great Uncle Tully sinks his claws into the car seat

young couple would live all those years later.

When they arrived at Bridgewater House, Richard showed Tullius each room and the cat familiarised himself by careful sniffing. First they entered the hallway with the cool, tiled floor and wooden panelling leading to a polished wooden staircase. On either side of the hallway there is a door. Behind one is a dining room, which receives a lot of natural light and leads to the conservatory. Behind the other is a sitting room with a fireplace covered in painted blue and white tiles. Two big chairs, covered in green velvet with high backs and big round arms, face the fireplace.

If you pass the staircase, you will find yourself in a kitchen with daffodil yellow walls and an old, rectangular

porcelain sink held up by wooden cupboards. A wooden plate rack is fixed on one of the walls, with small hooks underneath, where cups and mugs hang down. There is also a long, oblong piece of wood fixed horizontally to the wall that has meat hooks screwed in to it. From these hooks, all sorts of large scale kitchen utensils hang off – a spatula and long fork for turning meat for a summer barbecue, an enormous potato masher and a giant straining spoon.

"This all seems rather large for one man," Tullius mused.

"Yes I suppose it is," Richard replied. "I came to the house with many things left in it. I suspect quite a large family used to live here, and very little has changed since then. I bought the house from an old lady who might have been the last of the family. She wanted to sell everything and move as little as possible. I like it because the house has a history and is full of memories. It helps me write being in a place where people have lived for a long time and left a little hint of themselves behind."

They climbed the stairs to the second level where there were two bedrooms. The writer paused for a moment – should he give Tullius his own room? The day was getting stranger still. As was to become their custom, he asked Tullius what he thought.

"Well, I am pleased to be offered my own territory as I am not used to sharing. Usually I find the place I feel most comfortable myself, but let us see if I am happy here."

Richard opened the door to the guest room and in went the cat. Tullius immediately jumped up on the bed to see if it would make a good sleeping spot.

"Would you like to see the rest of the house now?" asked Richard.

They went next to Richard's room, then up to the final floor where there was a single room that ran the length and breadth of the house. It was very light with its six windows, and quite warm. The room was fairly empty apart from a mahogany desk with a leather work-surface, a lamp, a computer and a notepad. Each wall was patterned by the grids of light and shadows caused by the windows with their six leaded panes.

"This is where I do most of my work. Is there anything you would like me to get you to make you feel more at home?" Richard asked.

"Perhaps there could be something in here where I could rest comfortably?"

The writer found some large cushions and arranged them on the floor. They could often be found in that room – Tullius on his cushions, sleeping with his paws twitching as he dreamt of catching mice, and the man gently tapping the keys of the computer, sometimes into the early hours. And then Tullius would wake up and begin his night adventures, exploring in the darkness the garden surrounding the canal and sometimes going as far as Ashridge Park – where he saw deer speckled white and an ancient beech tree forest.

Before long the writer started calling Tullius "Tully", as it was easier to say and more familiar, and so it happened that his great nephew, ten years later, was not the only cat in the family to be called by this name.

And now I need to tell you the Ancient Cat Secret, but I hope you will keep it a secret as Richard the writer did. You may have wondered how it was that Bess overheard the human's talking of Bagheera's kittens' departure or how Juno understood what the Parisien editor of the lifestyle magazine was saying. The answer is that it was not just Great Uncle Tully who could understand and speak with humans – all cats have these abilities…it's just that some choose not to use them and others don't know they have them! I will explain this more later. First let me tell you how it was that Great Uncle Tully decided to break the unspoken rule between those cats that know they have these abilities – that they must never reveal them to humans.

Richard often commented on how amazing it was that this cat could speak with him but no others could, and often pondered on how it could possibly be explained. Great Uncle Tully saw the writer thinking it over again and again, like a plot in one of his novels. In the beginning this amused him, and he smiled quietly to himself. He also knew that, as a cat, he had a duty not to tell him as he might risk the welfare of his fellow cats if other humans came to know through Richard. He had already taken a huge liberty by speaking with this one man, but he had reasoned that the writer was very solitary and his long

observation of him during the summer suggested he could trust him. But as they spent more and more time together, and enjoyed that time, he found that he wanted to tell him the whole truth.

One wintry night about two years after Great Uncle Tully had moved into the cottage, when they were sitting by the fire in the green velvet armchairs after a good dinner, he sat upright and stared intensely at Richard.

"What's the matter, Tully, can you hear something?" Richard had become accustomed to the cat's acute hearing where the slightest noise outside might alert him.

"No, I have something to tell you of great importance, and you must understand that I do you a great honour in giving you this information. You must not pass it on." Richard nodded and Tully continued.

"Cats, as you yourself have observed, are clever creatures, and cats that choose to live with humans are often the brightest cats of all. These cats (my ancestors) allowed themselves to become domesticated so that they could live in comfort.

"In fact, I originally lived with humans and was happy living on their farm until the wife of the man died. The farmer married another woman, who mistreated me, so I left and decided to live the life of a wild cat, until I met you. I haven't spoken about this before because I try to forget it.

"My ancestors wanted to ensure that they led a life of leisure, doing pretty much what they wanted, when they

wanted. They realised that it was essential that humans did not know that cats could understand and speak to them, as they would give their cats various household tasks to do. So that is how the Ancient Cat Secret came about – domesticated cats decided to conceal their ability to understand and communicate with humans in order to lead a quieter and more relaxing existence.

"As this has been happening for generations, it has led to some interesting side effects. Many cats do not know that they have the ability to speak to their owners and so don't develop it. As far as understanding and listening to humans is concerned, they have what is called 'selective hearing'. This means that these cats only overhear what humans are saying if it is relevant to them in some way.

"There are also cats that are aware of their abilities to both understand and speak to humans, but they often choose to switch off from human conversation in any case. You see Richard," Tully paused, "to be blunt, these cats – present company excepted! – do not find human conversation particularly interesting. They feel that there is an awful lot of it... why will the occasional miaow not do?" Richard laughed. "Body language and sounds are much more important ways of conversing to us. Cats say a lot with their eyes, paws, tails... when the hairs stand up on their backs. And they love silence. We don't usually need to speak, and so human's conversation sounds like..." Tully hesitated, "Like a lot of noise really, and cats like as little noise as possible."

And there it was: the Ancient Cat Secret. Perhaps your cat can understand and speak to you but may not realise it can?

About eight years passed in the house by the lock in Berkhamsted, and Great Uncle Tully led a unique life where he was treated with the equal respect and allowed to make his own decisions. In return for his company the man provided him with food and comfort, and once again hunting became a pleasure for him rather than a necessity.

One evening Richard told Tully that he had drawn up a will so that, should anything happen to him, his house and his savings would go to his cat. He wanted to be sure that Tully could live the independent but comfortable life he had lived so far, and he worried that if Tully had to go back to hunting he might not manage it now. He was growing old and was no longer as trim as when Richard had met him – many good dinners had been had by both since then! The will stated that a certain amount of unwrapped fresh meat should be delivered every other day from the local butchers Eastwood, who would be paid weekly by direct debit. This way, the cat would have no trouble finding the food. The butcher, Joe, should top up the large water bowls from the outdoor tap. Richard knew that Joe would find this a very surprising request, but he knew that the butcher was a good man and very honest with his customers. Great Uncle Tully listened and thanked him but it seemed a far-off prospect. Sadly, only two years later Richard's arrangements were required.

So Great Uncle Tully became a cat of his own means –

you might say he was a cat aristocrat living by his inheritance! He missed Richard and began to think of what would happen when he, too, passed away. Would he be the last cat to live like this?

A plan began to form in his mind: was it possible he could trust and approach the solicitor who had drawn up Richard's will, and ask the solicitor to do the same for him, now that the house was his? If he could, who would he give the house to? Cats did not generally think in terms of relatives as once they were taken to different homes, at a very young age, they usually never saw each other again.

Tully had the advantage that he had been taken from the cottage in Chorley Wood at about four months old, rather than the usual eight weeks, and so he remembered where he had been born with his sister, Bagheera's mother, Bess. Like Juno, he too had not travelled far to his first owners and knew the area around Chorley Wood well.

It was a very big task, but he thought this was his only hope: he must walk the long distance from Berkhamsted to the cottage. Some of his relatives might still be there, and Great Uncle Tully would know what to do after he found out. While it was an hour in a car, he would have to make the trip walking on his paws. He would have to hunt, as it would probably take several days there and back. He felt in good health but he knew that at his age (he was thirteen years old which is elderly for a cat) it would take him much longer than in the years before he had met Richard. In terms of the route from

Berkhamsted to Chorley Wood, he was reasonably confident of that, since he and Richard had often gone a fair bit of the way before on their long walks together.

Chapter Five

A week later, after planning carefully and filling himself with as much of the butcher's meat as possible, Great Uncle Tully set off. It was an early summer day in June. He was a little apprehensive about surviving the journey, but he reasoned that his end would come sometime or other. It was better to attempt the noble task of leaving his inheritance to his kin than to pass his last days in the house having given up on his dream.

He travelled by day and night, stopping for an hour to rest now and then. Once on the journey he reflected that it might be a bit unrealistic to use his hunting skills – his reaction and speed, which were so critical in catching prey, were bound to be so much slower and might expend most of his energy without any result. Therefore he must travel as far and as quickly as possible while the food in his stomach lingered.

There were several times when he was unsure of which direction to take and had only his instincts to guide him. The smells of the forest of Chorley Wood were different to those of the canal town and Ashridge Park… he sniffed the air trying to identify the different elements. It was four days before Great Uncle Tully saw the silhouette of the cottage. His paws and legs ached mightily with the effort. His stomach felt

like a yawning gap. When he saw the light streaming from the diamond panes in the arched windows, he knew this was the cottage of his birth.

The window by the green velvet sofa with the curling arms was open, and he heaved himself up on to the ledge to look in. Below him he could see two female cats curled up together on the sofa and two large dogs, in their respective dog baskets, at either side of the room. There was a clatter of plates and the sound of running water coming from the kitchen. He decided he must go in now, as the window might be shut later. It was important the humans did not see him in case they shooed him away - he did not have the strength to deal with that. With a last effort he jumped down onto the sofa.

Bess and Bagheera scattered and stood blinking next to George in his dog basket. The hair on their backs was standing on end and their tails had become wide, bushy wands. They waited to see if this was an aggressive intruder. Great Uncle Tully was careful to sit quietly with his ginger tail curled neatly around his feet, blinking slowly at them – this conveyed to them that he was not there to challenge their territorial rights. Several minutes passed and none of the cats moved.

Then Great Uncle Tully miaowed quietly and said, "I was born in this cottage and I have come to seek my descendants." He looked at Bess wondering if there was a family resemblance.

Bess remembered that there was a ginger kitten in her

litter who stood out from the rest and was the last to go. "I am thirteen years old. How old are you?" she asked.

"I am thirteen also," said Tully. "Do you think we came from the same litter?"

And they both walked around examining each other. He noticed his sister's eyes were jade green like his, which is very unusual to find in a ginger cat. She noticed this too, but there was something much more powerful that proved they were siblings. It is difficult to describe but they both had a strong sense – maybe not a smell exactly – but so strong that it felt as if it was. There was a brief pause and then at the same moment they gave each other a tender lick behind the ear.

"You are brother and sister!" said Bagheera.

"This is my daughter Bagheera, and I am Bess. I was very fortunate to remain with one of my children and also our mother, Izzie, who has, I am sorry to tell you, passed away now."

"I am Tullius, or Tully for short. I am sad to hear of our mother but did she live to a ripe old age?"

"Yes, indeed she did – it is only a year since she left us."

"And how old are you Bagheera?" Tully turned his attention to the younger cat.

"I am seven years old."

"Have you had any children?" But with these words his voiced suddenly faded. All his strength was gone and he slumped on the sofa.

"We must let him rest," said Bess, her whiskers twitching with concern. "We must leave some food from our bowls for him to eat in the morning".

They all slept on the sofa that night, with Bess and Bagheera together at one end and Great Uncle Tully at the other. When dawn came, he woke up and crawled behind the sofa with his belly on the cold flagstones – this way he would not be found by the humans. Later in the morning when the way was clear, he joined Bess and Bagheera who had smelled his presence even though he had been out of sight. It reminded Bagheera of the smell of the feral male, the father of her children. She wondered why her uncle felt the need to travel so far and exhaust himself to find out about relatives that he had either left long ago or never met. This was strange behaviour indeed for a cat.

She showed him to the milky muesli mix in their food bowls, and he ate greedily. Then he quickly lapped up some water and felt himself once again. Although he still felt hungry, Bagheera told him there would be mince for lunch which he would find more substantial than the muesli.

They went outside, under a shady tree well hidden from the cottage, to share the little knowledge they had of their relatives. Apart from Izzie, Bess, Bagheera and Great Uncle Tully, no one knew where any other relatives might be – all had been taken away by strangers with no trace left behind… except, that is, Tully and Juno. And this is where we return to their story.

Juno, you will remember, had been taken by a lady from Chorley Wood. She knew the humans that owned the cottage in a neighbourly way. They were aware that she had moved to Paris and that Juno had gone with her, and they still exchanged Christmas cards. It was the previous year's Christmas card that gave the exciting news of Juno's modelling career. Bagheera and Bess had used their selective hearing to good effect when they had heard the humans talk about Juno to a visitor. Bagheera felt very proud and longed to see a modelling picture of her daughter.

But there was also news of Tully. After the first few weeks in Berkhamsted, the couple from Bedford Street had (unusually) sent a photograph of him lounging on the sofa. They had written a brief note about how he was settling in, and included their names and address on the back of the photograph.

The card and photograph meant so much to Bagheera. She knew that she was particularly fortunate to have known her own mother and grandmother, and so had accepted that she would probably never know the whereabouts of her offspring. When she learned the fates of two of her kittens, it was an unexpected and much valued gift. And so it was that Great Uncle Tully's heirs were identified.

There was no question of Bagheera leaving the cottage to begin a new life. It was a beautiful place that she shared with her mother, and it had been her home for many years. Tully was secretly pleased, as he had imagined giving his

inheritance to a younger cat who would be able to adapt easily to a life without human control. When he heard that Bagheera's son was called Tully, he swelled with pride at the thought that his name would continue to another generation. Richard would also have found it fitting that the name he had picked would carry on. It was even better still if both Tully and Juno would inherit the house together – a brother and sister reunited and supporting each other in their independence!

The first question now was how Great Uncle Tully could contact them – if indeed the solicitor agreed to make the will. The second question was: would they accept their inheritance and leave their present homes behind them?

Great Uncle Tully explained to Bagheera that, if he could succeed in getting the solicitor to make the will, he would need the card and the photograph to contact Tully and Juno. He sensed her reluctance to part with them. "I thank you, Bagheera. I will send you word whatever happens and some way or other return these to you."

First she retrieved the card with Juno's picture. She had, a little guiltily – knowing this was against the house rules – jumped on to the mantelpiece and knocked the card on to the floor before New Year. She had then pushed it under the far corner of the sofa as a hiding place so that there was something of Juno she could keep. The address was stamped in gold inside.

The photograph of Tully was not so easy to obtain,

and again involved breaking the house rules. Bagheera had to leap on to the kitchen table and then on to the sink, before edging her way around to the windowsill that would be her support. She placed one of her front paws, with claws out, around the edge of the photograph and began to ease it away from the blue-tack that stuck it to the kitchen cupboard. As it fluttered to the floor, she jumped back down and carried it gently in her mouth to her uncle in the sitting room.

Luckily Bagheera had left no paw prints on the sink, as she had cleaned her feet well beforehand. Shortly afterwards, the humans returned to the house and went into the kitchen. The cats heard the clink of food bowls being prepared with lunch. Bess and Bagheera quietly agreed to leave their lunch for Great Uncle Tully, so that he could have a good meal before he travelled the long distance back to Berkhamsted. He thanked them for their generosity – every morsel was a piece of energy that would carry him home. His muscles were aching but the news of Tully and Juno lifted him up. He was keen to return as soon as possible and implement the next stage of his plan.

After lunch Bess and Bagheera washed Great Uncle Tully from tip to toe as a parting ritual of affection. He was quite dirty from his travels and had not the strength to wash himself. Seedpods, stalks and mud were all extracted from his shaggy fur, which was then licked and smoothed. He was a little grey around the whiskers, but otherwise his dark ginger colour remained, and the grooming brought out its deep richness.

Chapter Six

It was a Friday evening and Mr Humphrey Beadle was getting ready to go home when he heard a scraping sound coming from the back of the office. The office was at the lower end of Berkhamsted's High Street in a Tudor-style building with white plaster walls, criss-crossed with black wooden beams and high pointed eaves. Hanging from a metal bracket there was a swinging sign with gold, peeling lettering saying "Castle Chambers". Mr Beadle was looking forward to his retirement and had just another month or so before all his clients' business was either completed or passed on to another solicitor. It was he who had been entrusted with drawing up the writer Richard Lebowski's will.

"There it is again that scraping sound... what could it be?" he wondered as he put his calculator and pens into the draw of the large mahogany desk. He picked up his coffee mug and walked into the back of the office, where there was a kitchenette with a kettle, a fridge and a small side window. It was still very light outside and he was surprised to see a large, ginger paw scraping on the glass.

He peered down to see a cat, Richard's cat no less, balancing on a dustbin and reaching up with his paw. Opening the window to shout at the cat, he stuck his head out a little

and banged it against the frame.

Tully's words rang out, almost as if they were in Mr Beadle's head (like it had been with Richard in the cottage in the forest): "Forgive me, Mr Beadle, for disturbing you but I need to talk to you on a very important matter." Tully knew how absurd this must have sounded to Mr Beadle and banging his head had not been the start he had hoped for. "Could I come inside for a moment where we can talk more easily?"

Mr Beadle stepped back from the window in a daze and leant against the wall. He pulled a chequered handkerchief out of his pocket to wipe his spectacles. Tully leapt in and walked through to the office and jumped on to the mahogany desk, hoping Mr Beadle would follow him.

"We could talk more comfortably in here, sir," he said with all the authority and confidence he could summon.

"Can this really be happening?" the solicitor wondered out loud, and then found himself sinking back into the leather chair next to desk.

"Have you ever thought about Richard Lebowski's will and why he left all his money and his house to his cat?"

"Yes I have," Humphrey found himself replying. "It was a strange will, but Mr Lebowski was not your average kind of chap, being an author and all that."

"And do you know that I am his cat and so the house and money belong to me?"

"Yes, I see you are he. Richard insisted that I come to see you, I remember, so that I could be sure to enforce the will

should there be any challenges to it."

"Well, I am growing old now and I do not know how much time I have left. I have one wish, which is to pass on my inheritance to my descendants. I have identified two cats whose addresses I have." Great Uncle Tully paused to see if he was going too quickly for Humphrey.

Humphrey opened the bottom draw of the desk and pulled out a bottle of whisky and a tumbler and poured in a large measure.

"If the house and money is legally mine… which you agree it is?" Tully paused.

"Yes, it is legally yours, although if someone were to challenge I cannot say what would happen. However, no one has challenged it so far, and it looks unlikely that anyone would."

"Well then, surely I can have a will made also, so that I can pass on the inheritance to my relatives?"

Humphrey took a deep breadth and peered at Tully over his spectacles. Was this all an illusion brought on by banging his head? He touched the desk – yes, it felt solidly real, and then he touched his arm, yes that was there too. There was nothing for it, he must carry on with this bizarre reality! "Well, in theory, I think that is possible. I will have to check to be sure."

"Will you help me do this?"

There followed a short silence.

"Yes, as Mr Lebowski's inheritor I will help you, as it seems broadly in line with his wishes." On a less serious note

Humphrey added, "Well I never!"

Humphrey then took some legal books down from the shelves, flicking through the pages to see if there was anything that specifically forbade the making of a will for a cat, but there was nothing to be found. Tully showed him the photograph and Christmas card, which Bagheera had curled up and hung from string from his collar. They discussed how the younger Tully and his model sister could be contacted. Mr Beadle suggested he write a letter to Juno's owner. The letter he produced (which is copied below) was not strictly honest, and therefore something he would never normally do. But it was the only way they could expect a reply from Juno's owner – the whole truth being much too strange for her to accept. Mr Beadle sent the letter that very week.

Contacting his great nephew would be far more simple than his great niece, as the younger Tully lived only minutes away from Bridgewater House. Great Uncle Tully would simply find him and explain the opportunity that lay before him.

As Great Uncle Tully went home that evening, the second question was foremost in his mind. Would either Tully or Juno want to leave their current lives behind and live at the house as independent cats with no owners? After all, they had been brought up by humans since they were eight weeks old. He had had longer than them to learn cat ways before he was taken to the farm. He had then lived as a wild cat, and now desired and needed his independence, but would they share his

desire? Even if Juno wanted to come, how likely was it that her owner would let her go, and if so, how would Juno travel from France? These questions and many more kept Great Uncle Tully awake that night and he came to the conclusion, by the time that the sun began to rise, that his whole plan was really rather incredible. He sighed deeply. But then he smiled to himself – had he not lived an incredible life, and if you did not have a dream what was life all about anyway?

Mr Humphrey Beadle
Solicitor
84 High Street
Berkhamsted
Herts HP4 2EN
e-mail: beadle@solicitor.org.uk

Dear Ms Leticia Mills

I am writing to you concerning a very unique command made in the will of Mr Richard Lebowski of Bridgewater House. He asked that his house be made into a refuge for cats and that they be provided with food out of his savings. In particular he mentioned that any cats originating from the cottage in Chorley Wood, where you purchased your cat Juno from, were most welcome. Should you ever have occasion, through some unforeseen circumstance, to need to find another home for Juno, I do hope you will contact me on this number straight away: +44 (0) 1442 684512.

Yours sincerely

H Beadle

H Beadle

Chapter Seven

The letter struck the doormat lightly, but loud enough for Madame Mills (formerly of Chorley Wood) to leave her breakfast and collect the post. There it was – only one letter in a printed, stiff, cream envelope. She took it back to the breakfast table and sliced it open with a knife.

Juno was picking, with little excitement, at dry cat food in her bowl in the kitchen. Her diet had changed dramatically in the last few weeks. No longer did she have a diet of the richest pickings in return for the glamour and money she brought to the household. She would not like me to say this, being very concerned to keep up an elegant appearance at all times, but the truth is that Juno had begun to be sick fairly regularly and did not always make it to the apartement's litter tray in time. There had also been a couple of embarrassing experiences while modelling when she had suddenly felt very ill while posing for the photographer, and knew she had to stay very still... but the lamps were hot and she felt more and more queasy till finally she found herself letting out the most amazing cat noise. You might even say it sounded like a siren: "Whaaaaohhhwhaaaohhhhwhaaaaa!"

Madame Mills had taken her to the vets after it happened the second time, and was asked what she fed Juno.

When she answered that Juno ate sirloin steak, devilled eggs and crème brulée, the vet was very sharp with her.

"This cat has a delicate stomach and is very stressed. It is possible that the stomach condition is causing the stress but it could be some other cause. My advice is: feed her on dry cat food granules and water only – absolutely no cream or anything like it, and examine your lifestyle together. Think about whether there is anything that might be causing her stress. You should find that she will very rarely be sick if she sticks to this diet and leads a calm life."

Madame Mills was somewhat put out – she tried to explain how she was rewarding the cat and letting her share in the best of her life, but the vet would have none of it. She and Juno left as quickly as possible.

So when Madame Mills read the letter from Mr Beadle, things were not as rosy as they had once been for Juno. Her diet had become very plain indeed (although she had to admit she was feeling a lot better for it) and the modelling jobs seemed to come fewer and farther between. Perhaps word had got around about her being sick during photo-shoots, or maybe it was simply that she had been photographed many times now – there were other cats to take her place to give a different look and readers always wanted to see something new. She did not miss the pressure of the work, but she did miss the attention as it made up for her loneliness. I expect she would say now that at that time she sought to impress others, rather than extend her paw in friendship. She did not have any friends, just other

animals she met at photo-shoots or at the chic cafés and restaurants she accompanied her owner to, and they were all a bit like her – very elegant but a little cold, a little judging.

Madame Mills had been worrying for the last few weeks about what to do with Juno over the next three months. She was planning a long holiday, travelling around Italy, but she suspected that the people who fed Juno when she was usually away would not accept the task for that amount of time. And there had been all this cat sick to clean up – what would happen to the apartement if she was away? She could send Juno to the cattery, but it was expensive and she wondered how Juno would react to being in a strange place with lots of other animals for that amount of time. After the recent trip to the vets, she worried that a cattery would be too stressful.

She saw Juno padding back into the room, and with a twinge of sadness everything seemed to suddenly make sense. Juno might be better off at Bridgewater House: certainly a long journey would be better than the cattery? Also, Madame Mills would no longer have the responsibility of a cat (which she had to admit was becoming less appealing by the day). She noticed there was an e-mail address at the top of the letter and, with no more thought, went to the study to e-mail Mr Beadle and ask him if he could meet the Eurostar train at Waterloo and, for a fee, drive Juno back to Bridgewater House himself. So once again Juno's destiny relied on that of her owner, but at least this time there was a permanent home waiting for her.

It was around nine o'clock on the same morning

(10 o'clock French time), on the same day that Madame Mills had received the letter about Juno, that Tully was sunbathing in the garden at his home in Bedford Street. At that time of day, lying in the sun made his fur warm (but not hot), which was very pleasant. In another hour or so he would set off to explore the other gardens, and see whether any of his human friends in the nearby houses had a nice titbit for him. He returned home for his lunch of dry cat granules that was usually served at half-twelve or one o'clock. Then, with a full belly, Tully would take a long afternoon nap in the upstairs bedroom – the sock draw had become a little cramped so he had moved to the king size bed! When he heard the turn of the key in the front door, he would appear at the top of the stairs to greet his owners. After dinner was served, he would often sit between the couple enjoying being stroked and, if there was tennis or football on, watch the television – seeing the ball bounce around was quite entertaining. He would follow the couple to bed and sleep at the bottom of it until the early hours of the morning, when he left soundlessly to hunt and then returned before they were awake.

On Fridays there was one variation to Tully's day. The manager of the Old Mill Inn, which was a few minutes gallop from Bedford Street, had become one of his human friends. Tully had followed the tasty food smells coming from the Inn and often whisked his way ahead of someone who had opened the door. He had become a kind of "regular" (as they like to term people who visit the same café, inn or restaurant often).

In recognition of Tully's status, the manager had one day given him a small amount of their homemade beef and Theakston pie and a small saucer of creamy liquid that was in fact the top of a beer called Guinness. The two were a delicious combination, and Tully spent a great deal of his time washing himself afterwards – which is how you know whether cats have enjoyed their meal. He decided to turn up at the same time and day the following week, which was about 4 o'clock on a Friday when the pub was very quiet. To get the manager's attention he sat on one of the tall, ladder-back wooden chairs with a square seat looking expectantly for his dinner, which was then placed next to him. And so that was how it came to be that Tully would sit in the Old Mill every Friday and have his beef and Theakston pie and his Guinness brought to him. The couple never could quite understand why he did not seem bothered about his food on a Friday night – there was no miaowing in the kitchen when they returned home. He would just lie on his back on the sofa, like a starfish, allowing as much space for his tummy as possible.

Tully was on his way to the Old Mill Inn the Friday following his great uncle's visit to Mr Beadle. He had gone down the canal path, over the humpback bridge and was heading the short distance down the road to the inn, when a large ginger cat ran up behind him and trotted alongside. Tully looked across at him searching for signals of intent – was he somehow invading this cat's territory or was the cat being friendly? And then something happened that he had never

experienced before: he heard his name ringing out, almost as if it was in his own head.

"Tull...y!" cried out the ginger cat using human language. Tully stood still and stared. Great Uncle Tully then changed back to cat language and said, with various miaows, twitching of his paws, tail and eye movements, "I need to speak to you. I'm your great uncle, also called Tully. I have important news!"

This was a shock to him – like most domesticated cats separated at eight weeks from their brothers and sisters, he had not given his family a thought. But Tully was a very friendly and gentle cat and simply said, "Why not come with me to the Old Mill and share some food?"

So off they went together and the manager found two large, shaggy cats, one ginger and one black and white, waiting for him on the ladder-back chair that day! After sharing the creamy beer and the beef pie and cleaning their whiskers and paws, Great Uncle Tully explained the whole story of how he had met Richard and was now the owner of a fine property constantly supplied with food and water. Tully's eyes widened as he heard of the fresh meat being delivered from Eastwood – the best butcher in Berko no less! He had feasted on an Eastwood goose leg the previous Christmas and he had rated it as his ultimate food experience so far. But he was puzzled at his great uncle living at Bridgewater House, on his own with no human companionship.

"Well I have to say I miss Richard. We were very close,

but humans like him are few and far between. No one else would give me the freedom he gave me whilst enjoying the comforts of his home. And what about your owners, what are they like?" Great Uncle Tully asked.

Tully described the affection he received from the couple, including the massaging of his head and the scratching of his lower back (which he particularly liked), that they often played together and the fondness he felt for them.

"I see Tully - it is a good life you have…" said his great uncle, a little sadly, as he realised his offer might not be as appealing as he had thought. "And what would you say if I offered you my house with the money and food that goes with it to be yours forever?"

"Where are you going?" asked Tully, concerned now that he might lose his great uncle's company after only just meeting him.

"Nowhere immediately, but you may not realise that I am thirteen years old now. I need to think about what will happen to my inheritance when I am gone. I want to leave the house to you and to your sister, who I am presently trying to contact. I would like you both to live there now, so that I can have the contentment of seeing my family there before I pass on."

Tully listened and paused while he was taking in his great uncle's words. He immediately felt a huge ache inside at the thought of leaving his home in Bedford Street – the couple had been his family since he was eight weeks old. He was

happy where he was. But he wanted to please his great uncle and he knew it was a grand offer indeed. "I would like to accept your offer but I can't bear the thought of leaving where I am. Yet I am so glad to have met you. Now we can get to know each other and I can easily come and visit you at Bridgewater House."

"Tully, I understand I am pulling you away from what you know but think about what I am offering you! You and your sister have the opportunity to live like no other cats, apart from myself, have lived before. To live like a human with all the comforts and securities of life but be completely free – a master of your own destiny! I know this is difficult. We cats are inclined to think as single entities – we are separated from our family at such an early age so that family and freedom seem to mean little when we grow up. We accept our place in the human scheme of things without question and many humans are good owners. But think – you are not just a pet, you are a noble cat!"

Tully sat quietly for a moment. "I am sorry but I am a cat who likes the life I lead. I see no reason to change it. What difference will it make to other cats if I leave Bedford Street and live in Bridgewater House? Please let us leave the matter here," he said looking up at his great uncle with his tender, pale green, eyes. Great Uncle Tully sighed and put his chin down on the wooden seat. He felt deflated. "But, uncle, there is still my sister you spoke of – your dream might still be realised in her!"

"Yes, that is true. But it is altogether more unlikely that she will be able to come to Bridgewater House, as she lives in another country."

"Tell me about her," said Tully excitedly. "Where does she live? Does she have a name? I will have a great uncle and maybe a sister too, living nearby!"

Great Uncle Tully sat up again and shook off his downcast mood. He explained where Juno was living and as much as he knew of her life in Paris. "She sounds nothing like me at all," mused Tully. He was having difficulty imagining a cat modelling and living in a big city.

That night Great Uncle Tully and his great nephew went back to their respective homes. Tully was excited at the events of the day and kept running back and forth from the garden to the kitchen to the lounge, as he had when he was a young kitten. "What is up with him tonight?" said the couple to each other.

Great Uncle Tully felt tired but was beginning to get over his disappointment. At least he had tried and, after all, it was Tully's decision and he had to accept it. Now that his mind was freer of his dream, he began to think about getting to know Tully – to know one of his family properly, closely for the first time.

Chapter Eight

The next week Great Uncle Tully had a very pleasant surprise. Mr Beadle came round to the house to explain he had received an e-mail from Juno's owner and she was being despatched from France the very next week. He said he would collect her and bring her back.

"Thank you so much, Humphrey. I can't tell you how much this means to me. Without you this could never have happened. I am always in your debt."

"Well I am pleased to have been truly amazed. There I was settling down to retire, a little bored with life and with no plans ahead, and you showed me that a whole other world exists. I have decided to travel to Mexico for a few weeks – I've often thought that it would be a wonderful place to visit, but I've never been."

"I am glad to hear that, Humphrey – we must all seize the day! I hope you will visit us when you return."

The day of Juno's arrival came, and what a strange day it was for her. She had no idea of what was going to happen – Madame Mills and Mr Beadle had communicated through letter and e-mail, and so she had not been able to use her selective hearing to find out what lay in store for her. Needless to say, it was very upsetting to be placed in her cat carrier and

left with the staff at the Paris Eurostar, placed in a special luggage hold which was quite dark, then catapulted to a new place. She huddled against the farthest wall of the cat carrier shivering with nerves. Why had her owner left her?

At Waterloo Mr Beadle signed the necessary documents and was given her pet passport. Then Juno swayed from side to side in her carrier as she was taken a short distance to his car. Mr Beadle, thinking that Juno might have the same special abilities that her Great Uncle Tully did, talked to her on the journey back. He explained where she was going, about her great uncle and her brother, and he described Berkhamsted and the location of the property. Juno heard all this and it soothed her, but she made no reply. Tully and Juno, along with almost all cats you will meet, did not realise they had the power of human speech. Finally the long day was at its end and the car stopped at Bridgewater House. Mr Beadle carried her box into the conservatory and shut the door, in case she decided to run away, and then called for Great Uncle Tully. Humphrey then undid the locks and the grill swung forward. He left them there together, with Juno huddled at the back and Great Uncle Tully peering in.

"Juno, I am your Great Uncle Tully. You are safe here. This is your home now and you are free to do as you will. Please come out and have a look around."

Juno saw his soft jade eyes and his concern, and moved out of the carrier. He took her through to a full water bowl and showed her the cat flap. He then felt it best to leave her

on her own for a while.

It was after a few days that Tully received an invitation to dinner at Bridgewater House. He had rushed round to the house the day after Juno arrived, but his great uncle had headed him off in the garden. Great Uncle Tully informed him that Juno had been saying very little and appeared anxious. He felt that it would be better to leave her for a while. Moving to a new country without any prior knowledge was a big change, and it would take her time to get used to it. Great Uncle Tully chose to have the dinner on the following Wednesday. Eastwood always delivered fresh beef mince that day, at around 6 o'clock, after they had closed the shop for the day.

Tully approached the house that evening as the sun was setting, casting a deep pink glow over the blue slate roof. The many windows became mirrors flashing the sun between them. He made his way through the canal garden, his fur brushing against the foxgloves, and the strong scent of lavender making his nose twitch. He stood by the conservatory door looking to see if anyone was there, and saw the door was slightly open. He padded in and was met by a new smell – the unfamiliar scent of Juno. He let out a large miaow to announce his arrival and his great uncle and sister appeared a moment later. Juno walked in daintily with her tail held very high, almost vertical like a rod, and with her tiny chin jutting upwards.

"Hello, Tully. This is Juno, and Juno this is Tully – you are brother and sister!"

There was a silence that felt extremely long. Tully

looked Juno up and down, and Juno looked Tully up and down. Both were thinking the same thing: "How can we be related?" There was Tully with his shaggy coat with lots of white fur, including that which sprouted out of his ears, his enormous bushy tail and big, pale green eyes. There was Juno, petite, short-haired and sleek, with a very slim tail that you could hold between two of your toes. She was black apart from the hidden, underarm hair and the hint of brown that you could only see in sunlight and she had amber eyes. Meeting her great uncle had been a similarly strange experience, but it had made more sense to her that they were so different as there were several generations between them.

"Well...,"said Great Uncle Tully bridging the silence, "perhaps we should have dinner." So they made their way to the back of the house where the food had been left, and Tully helped him rip apart the plastic bag and butcher's paper to reveal the mince. Great Uncle Tully used his paws to divide the meat into three portions, pushing them onto different flag-stones so that each cat could have their own platter. Eating with all cats is a serious business so there was no conversation, which was rather fortunate as I wonder if Tully and Juno would have known what to say to one another. Finally the meal and the paw and face cleaning was over, and they made their way into the sitting room.

Juno headed for the rug in front of the fireplace and Tully and their great uncle took up the two velvet green chairs.

"So what do you do here, Tully?" asked Juno.

"Well I go for walks, do a spot of hunting…," said Tully, confident that hunting would be a good subject for three cats to discuss.

"Doesn't sound very exciting."

"Ummm, well catching frogs can be very exciting." He went on to describe the hunting of a large frog the previous evening.

Juno looked away. She had been brought up as a city cat and hunting did not seem like a natural activity to her. Why hunt when your food came ready prepared in plastic bags and containers? She noticed that Tully's white paws and bushy tail were dirty – she had the distinct impression that he had been *rolling in the dust!* Tully began to feel a little uncomfortable, but it was not in his nature to take anyone down a peg or two.

"I would like hear about your modelling," he said generously.

Juno warmed to her topic. She told them about the first photo-shoot on the chaise longue, the catwalk show, the fine Paris dining… It sounded very impressive, as she intended it to.

"It is good you have seen the world," said Great Uncle Tully.

Juno yawned in response and declared she was still rather tired because of her recent journey on the Eurostar. (Tully did not know what this was but didn't feel like asking.) She then quickly said her goodbyes and trotted out of the

sitting room.

Tully sat quietly. "Juno's a little difficult to get to know," said his great uncle softly. "I don't feel I have got to know her at all since she arrived. I know of her life but not what she feels or thinks about it. But we shall see, we shall see. I am so glad to have her here – she is obviously a very bright cat and will know how to look after her inheritance."

"Well yes," Tully said a little hesitantly, "but I don't think she liked me very much!"

"Don't worry, Tully. Just because you are family doesn't mean you'll get on straightaway!" And with that Great Uncle Tully felt very tired and fell asleep.

Tully set off home and, as he pushed his way through the cat flap at Bedford Street, he looked forward to cuddling up on the sofa with the couple – to be with those who knew and loved him.

But there was a shock for him the following morning while he was eating his breakfast. The couple were in the kitchen discussing whether to leave Berkhamsted. It was clear that neither wanted to, but nonetheless the decision was made to go. Tully felt as if he had been knocked back by a very strong wind. He went up to the bedroom and lay stiffly on the bed with his head up, staring in front of him. He knew they would not leave him – they would take him with them wherever they went – and he loved them for this. Had he not met Great Uncle Tully, it was beyond question that he would have left with them. But now he had options and he took

some time to think them over. It made him feel sick to leave the couple, but he loved Berkhamsted. It was his home and no other place would be the same. His great uncle's words came ringing back to him: "A master of you own destiny!" He fell asleep exhausted with the upheaval of his thoughts. Over the next two days, Tully tried not to think about it and went about his normal routine, but he was not happy. The couple noticed that he seemed depressed... his usual bouncy step and miaow were absent. He slept for even longer periods than normal and was off his food. They were thinking of taking him to the vet. On the third day he knew what he must do, and set off to tell Great Uncle Tully that he would like to take him up on his offer of living in Bridgewater House.

Weeks passed before a large furniture van arrived at the house in Bedford Street. The couple had been packing their things into boxes for the last week and now it was time to leave. Tully's cat carrier was placed in the centre of the sitting room ready to be used at a moment's notice, but he had not been seen all morning. The last time the couple had seen him was at the end of their bed the night before. The van was loaded up by the removal men and wound its way up the street. The couple, who were supposed to leave with the van, continued to search for him. They called his name and banged his food bowl with a fork (which usually made him arrive in a moment). Eventually they left, accepting that all they could do was call their friends and hope Tully was found, so they could come and collect him.

Tully had arrived at Bridgewater House in the early hours while the couple were sleeping. He had walked up the bed and nuzzled each and they had given him a sleepy stroke and then he had left. When he arrived at his new home he sat in the sitting room and the urge to rush back swept over him again and again. He had wanted to tell them and explain why. (Tully now knew he had the ability to use human speech and Great Uncle Tully was teaching him to develop this). But his great uncle had said he could not use this new-found ability to speak to his owners. The more humans who knew, the greater the risk to cat society – and humans that he no longer lived with might feel more tempted than most to tell, and also would find it much harder to part with him.

So a new life (and a new family) began with Tully, Juno and Great Uncle Tully at Bridgewater House. Juno was in Richard's old room. Great Uncle Tully insisted that his great nephew take his bedroom, as he was finding the stairs too tiring to climb and would rather sleep in one of the armchairs. Secretly it also pleased him to see them both settled in their rooms – it was how he hoped it would be for many years after he had gone.

From Juno's room you can see the church spire and a little of the High Street and its cafés and restaurants. From Tully's there is a canal view. He was very pleased with this – now he could do some armchair viewing of the ducks, geese and herons. Yet it was clear from Tully's manner, his lack of customary bounce and the absent sparkle in his eye that he

was missing his human family.

Great Uncle Tully did all he could to make Tully feel as much at home as possible. He suggested that Tully used the dining room, which was largely unused by them all, as a Trophy Room where he could keep and display the trophies from his hunting – mainly dead frogs. Tully was excited about this – he had never been allowed to keep any of his frogs before – the couple had always removed them as quickly as possible.

Great Uncle Tully had also been keeping a careful eye on Juno, who had now identified her favourite spots in the house and taken a few short trips outside to explore the neighbourhood. This was a good sign that her anxiety had lessened. However, he did notice that her stomach was bloated and she seemed to feel sick quite often. Eventually he asked her why this was. She had not mentioned it, as she enjoyed fine food as you know and did not want to stop eating Eastwood's meat. But Great Uncle Tully was firm with her and arranged for Mr Beadle to contact a local supermarket who delivered large bags of dry cat food every month. They agreed she could eat Eastwood's meat once a week as a treat.

The Trophy Room was not popular with Juno, as she did not find the smell of drying frog skin, which drifted around the rest of the house, very pleasant. She also discovered that Tully liked some of the same sleeping spots as she did. There was, for example, a very comfortable window seat in the attic room that received a lot of sunshine and was always warm. Many times she would go up there for a sleep

and find Tully already there, sprawled across the seat on his back, showing off his shaggy tummy!

Tully did not wash himself as much as she did, and he was often muddy after hunting. The window seat was beginning to look a little worse for wear and a trail of muddy paw prints led from the conservatory to the kitchen and up the stairs. These are just a few of the things that irritated Juno, and Tully was completely unaware of it. He was an "easy-come, easy-go" kind of cat – he would accept anything of you and assumed you would do the same for him. Meal times with the three together became a little tense, with Great Uncle Tully trying to dissolve the atmosphere with some chatter about the weather.

By the time October came around, Great Uncle Tully had missed quite a few meals, saying that he had no appetite and needed to rest. After a week of this Juno asked if he was feeling unwell, but Great Uncle Tully said he just felt very, very tired. He was growing thin, and Juno took the unusual step of talking to her brother one day after breakfast. "I am worried about him. We should do something." She had grown fond of Great Uncle Tully in the last few months even if she had not shown it. He had been true to his word – she was safe here and she sensed his tender concern for her.

"What should we do?" asked Tully.

"Somehow we need to get a vet to take a look at him. One helped me when I was sick. We could ask Mr Beadle to arrange it. Can you speak human well enough yet?" she asked.

Tully sprawling on the window seat

Great Uncle Tully had been teaching them over the last few months how to use this ability, as he knew they might need it at some point in the future in order to keep their home running smoothly.

"I think so, but I've never tried it out on a human yet."

"You know this town much better than me. Do you think you could go and find him and speak to him?" She hoped he would say yes, as the prospect of doing this herself was very frightening.

"Yes, I will try. I think he lives up Ellesmere Road, which is not far from here. I can go up there and keep watch until I see him come out of one of the houses."

Tully set off immediately and placed himself up on the bank facing the houses halfway down, where he had a good view of most of the doors in the road. Luckily Mr Beadle had returned from his Mexican trip, and late that afternoon Tully spotted him and raced up behind him, to get inside his house before he closed the front door.

"Hello!" said Mr Beadle, surprised.

"Hello," said Tully a little out of breath and a little haltingly, as his human speech was quite underdeveloped.

"Tully, my great uncle, is ill – can you take him to the vet?"

Mr Beadle phoned St Johns' vet surgery, and made an appointment for six o'clock. He then drove round to Bridgewater House and collected Great Uncle Tully, who smiled weakly at him, but did not seem to able to speak to Mr

Beadle.

After a thorough inspection and the taking of a blood sample, the vet said that Great Uncle Tully would need to be kept in overnight. He was very dehydrated and needed a saline drip to ensure his body replaced the lost moisture and salt. Mr Beadle would come back the following lunchtime for the results. He returned to Bridgewater House to tell Tully and Juno what was happening.

They spent an anxious night wondering what the next day would bring. Finally they heard the tap on the conservatory door and knew Mr Beadle had returned. He looked very sad. "I am afraid it is very bad news… very bad news," he repeated as he crumpled into a chair. "The vet told me there is nothing to be done for him. He has developed a condition where his red blood cells are no longer generating themselves, and this is stopping him from breathing properly. It will only get worse." He looked up from the floor and looked into the eyes of the two cats. "The vet has advised me to have him *put to sleep* as soon as possible, as he will only suffer a lot otherwise – at the moment he is in no pain."

Tully and Juno were weak with the news. Mr Beadle knew that he must persuade them that putting their great uncle to sleep was for the best. He had asked for a moment alone with Great Uncle Tully in the examination room after the vet had explained the situation. "You heard all that didn't you old boy?"

"Yes" said Great Uncle Tully in a voice so quiet, it was

like a wisp of air.

"It is your decision, not mine. What do you want me to do?"

"Bring Tully and Juno here tomorrow for me to see them one last time. Then tell the vet it is time." And with that he collapsed into sleep.

By the next day, his eyes had changed colour from their pale green to a dark brown and his breathing was hardly noticeable. But he purred when he saw Tully and Juno, and looked at them with his usual tenderness. There were many tears shed and much nestling into his fur. When it was time to leave, Great Uncle Tully summoned all his strength for one last act. He sat upright and with his front paws guided their front paws together, so that they touched. "Look out for each other" were his last words.

Chapter Nine

Tully and Juno returned home and both were very quiet. Neither felt much like eating and they retired to their bedrooms for the rest of the day. Next morning at breakfast it was difficult to know what to say and after that meal they ate at different times. This was partly a natural development. Great Uncle Tully had insisted that they all eat together, but Tully and Juno were never hungry at the same time, so this always proved a bit difficult to organise. Now he was not there to arrange it, they soon slipped into eating separately and more and more they stuck to different areas of the house. Tully tried to be as unseen and unheard as possible, because he assumed that Juno wanted to be on her own, and she in her turn did not know how to approach him. She had built up such a frosty exterior that if she reached out she felt she might suddenly turn to water and dissolve into nothing.

And so the autumn passed and the winter began in this manner. Even their first Christmas Day at Bridgewater House ended up the same – well it almost did.

The town of Berkhamsted had been experiencing a deep frost for several days. Each branch, twig and blade of grass wore a feathery-white fringe. Windowpanes were double-glazed with ice, and the pavements and tarmac roads

had become skating rinks for the people and animals clambering their way along them. By Christmas Day the canal itself was frozen over, and it was quite a sight to see the ducks and geese sliding on their bottoms from one side to the other.

Juno had never seen snow and ice before – Paris had never been that cold when she had been there. She spent hours on the window seat in the attic room admiring the scene below. That night it began to snow heavily and the frozen canal was coated in its thick, white icing. The sky was jet black and the stars looked like the small diamante stones punched into her collar. Although it was very cold and her fur was short, she ignored her usual desire for warmth and went outside to experience the night firsthand. She walked along the canal and studied its white surface. It was like a glistening present waiting to be unwrapped. She touched its surface with her left front paw and then both her front paws. It felt gravely, not slippery, and seemed firm. And then Juno leapt out on to ice, merrily sprinting across its surface, her amber eyes glowing with the moonlight rippling across her coat.

Tully was dozing lightly in Great Uncle Tully's old armchair by the fire. There had been a special Eastwood's feast delivered on Christmas Eve – goose legs – and he had eaten a giant share, as Juno only had a small appetite. Suddenly he heard the most piercing cat shriek ringing out. His heart began to thump against his chest and all his hairs stood on end. He raced outside to see what was happening and heard the noise again, coming from the canal outside the house. He made out

the dark outline of some front paws scraping and realised it was Juno. She had fallen through the ice!

Tully leapt across to her and cried out, "Juno! Juno! listen to me. I will turn my back and put my tail over the side. You must stick your claws in as hard as you can and I will pull you out of the water."

And with that he whipped himself round and dropped his great, warm bushy tail into the freezing water and felt her claws like needles. He pushed forward with his shoulders and, little by little, edged forward and away from the bank, bringing Juno with him. I do not know how long it took before he had brought her back to land. He says it felt like several minutes and just when he felt he had no pulling power left, there she appeared beside him, sodden and dripping, shivering intensely with cold.

"Now you must run inside by the fire as quick as you can!" he ordered, and in they both raced.

He had never seen cat fur look like this before – every hair was weighed down with water. Despite being in front of the fire for some time, Juno did not seem to be getting dry. With his teeth he dragged a tea towel from the kitchen and rolled her around in it. When that was damp, he went upstairs and somehow managed to drag a duvet down from one of the bedrooms. He wrapped them both up inside it together, and felt her shaking against his belly. An hour or so passed and she was still cold through. Her head was lolling, hazy with shock. He wondered if she would survive this, and thought how sad it

would be to lose two of his family after such a short time of knowing them. He kept watch, worrying, as time passed, with one hour holding on and reaching out to the next.

Finally he woke up to find it was morning and that he had at some point given in to sleep. He could hear noise coming from the kitchen, and he walked in to see Juno preparing breakfast for both of them. The moment she saw Tully she rushed towards him and gave him a big hug and licked his face all over! Then they shared the remainder of the goose legs with some of Juno's dry food, and merry cat chatter passed between them. They made up for all the conversations they could have had in the last few months by talking for hours about Paris and Berkhamsted, hunting and modelling. Tully offered to take her on a nature tour of the area, and Juno offered to give him some grooming tips. It did not matter anymore that they were different – they had each other and that was the best Christmas present either could have.

Juno often thinks about that night and how Tully saved her life. She always remembers her Great Uncle Tully's words: "Look out for each other." And whenever she and Tully are curled up together, while she is awake and he asleep, she keeps a watchful eye over him, ready to protect should the need ever arise.

THE END.

ACKNOWLEDGEMENTS

I should like to thank several entities, human, feline and inanimate, for their help.

My dearly departed cats, Tully & Juno, inspired this story and the characters and mannerisms of their namesakes are based on them. Hopefully I have gone some way to making them immortal which is no more than they deserve. I must also pay tribute to the lovely town and environs of Berkhamsted, which were as inspiring as my cats.

To my husband Richard for believing in me, and being my first reader and editor. To Caroline Freaney for being gutsy enough to take on the creative challenge of doing the illustrations and for doing them so very well. To Sandra Smith for her customary flair in designing the book cover and setting the text. To Tricia Gilbert who offered excellent professional proof reading and editing skills. To my mother for being one of my first readers and a much needed investor at the right time. To Shirley Menary for telling me I should write the book. To Gerry Howe for providing enthusiastic advice and support on the publishing and printing of this book.

Don't miss the sequel!

To receive information about the next book
in the Tully and Juno series:

Please send your email address or postal details to:
Sparky Press
15 Bedford Street
Berkhamsted
HP4 2EN
e-mail: sarah@sarahmenary.demon.co.uk

?

Would you like to buy prints, cards or other items with Caroline Freaney's illustrations on them?

If so please let Sparky Press know by contacting us at:

Sparky Press
15 Bedford Street
Berkhamsted
HP4 2EN
e-mail: sarah@sarahmenary.demon.co.uk

The Tale of Tully and Juno

COLOURING BOOK

"the cottage with its white stone walls... old diamond shaped panes. White wooden trellises strung with rose plants..."

COLOURING BOOK

"Tully was black...his paws were all white...Juno's eyes... a dark amber...At first sight she seemed black, but there was a hint of chocolate brown...a dab of white fur in the centre of her chest."

✎ COLOURING BOOK

"Great Uncle Tully. . .was a little grey around the whiskers, but otherwise his dark ginger colour remained."

"Tully had a [black] coat [but]. . .His chest and belly were white and he had a pure white flash in the middle of his forehead that ran down his nose, above his mouth and across his cheeks. . .Around his pale green eyes, forehead and ears he was black again. . .His paws were all white. . ."